anythink

New Glasses

Adapted by Reika Chan

SCHOLASTIC INC.

Peppa, George, and Pedro Pony
are playing in the mud.

Pedro slips.

His glasses fly off!

Pedro cannot see well without his glasses.

Peppa finds the glasses.
She gives them to Pedro.

"Why do you wear glasses?"
Peppa asks.

"My daddy says I need glasses
to see well," Pedro replies.
His daddy is an eye doctor.

Peppa likes Pedro's glasses. She wants some, too.

Pedro has an idea. He'll give Peppa an eye test!

First, Peppa closes one eye.
"What do you see?" Pedro asks.
"I can see George!" Peppa
replies.

Pedro tells Peppa to close
both eyes.

With both eyes closed, Peppa
cannot see anything.

"You cannot see?" Pedro says.

Peppa goes to a real eye doctor for a test.

Pedro's daddy, Mr. Pony, is the doctor.

"Put these glasses on," Mr. Pony says.

Peppa reads the letters on a chart.

Then Peppa reads the numbers.
"Now I will check your results,"
Mr. Pony says.

While Peppa waits for her results, she tries out glasses with Mummy Pig.

Peppa finds a pair of rainbow glasses.
"These are funny!" Peppa says.

Peppa tries on black glasses.
"These are too big," she says.

Then Peppa finds heart-shaped glasses.
"I look fantastic!" she says.

Mr. Pony returns with the results.

"Good news!" he says. "Peppa
has perfect eyesight."

"Does that mean I don't need glasses?" Peppa asks.

"Correct," Mr. Pony says.

This is not good news for Peppa.

She really wants the heart-shaped glasses!

"Hmm," Mr. Pony says. He has an idea. "Well, you could get sunglasses!"

Peppa tries on heart-shaped
sunglasses.
"Fantastic!" she says.

Peppa wants it to be sunny
every day.
    Then she can always wear her
sunglasses!
    Peppa loves glasses.
    Everyone loves glasses!